Chastity Belt

SHOSHANNA EVERS

Chastity Belt
by Shoshanna Evers

Georgia Hearn has found the perfect way to make easy cash—performing an interactive BDSM-flavored stage show at the exclusive Gentlemen's Club. When handsome GC client Jonathan Syler goes up onstage and locks her into a chastity belt, it's all supposed to be part of the fun. But Jonathan makes it clear he won't be unlocking her anytime soon.

Now she's at his mercy—and has no choice but to see him again, since he holds the key to her pleasure. Literally.

Chastity Belt © 2011 Shoshanna Evers
Original published by Ellora's Cave Publishing, April 2011
Edited by Jillian Bell
Cover art by Rob Sturtz www.SelfPubBookCovers.com

Print book publication, 2nd edition, copyright © 2013 Shoshanna Evers

ISBN-10: 0988753782
ISBN-13: 978-0-9887537-8-5

DEDICATION

For my husband, always and forever.

CONTENTS

ACKNOWLEDGMENTS

Thank you to my readers, first and foremost. Without you, I would be writing into the abyss. And a special shoutout goes to the Shoshanna Street Team—thank you for your support, and for spreading the word!

Chastity Belt was originally published by Ellora's Cave Publishing in 2011. I'm grateful to them for letting me write all of the dirtiest fantasies that tickled my fancy, and for whipping my stories into shape. Thank you to Jillian Bell, who edited *Chastity Belt*.

It's a thrill to be able to re-issue this short novella, three years later, as a self-published book, at a low price for my readers. I'm grateful for the many indie authors who paved the way, showing me a path that has allowed me to be a full-time writer.

Thank you to my cover artist, Rob Sturtz, from SelfPubBookCovers.com for my new cover! I co-founded SelfPubBookCovers.com with Rob to help fulfill my dream of having quality covers at an affordable price available to all indie authors, instantly. If you're a writer, too, you might want to check out the amazing artists we have on board!

Last on the list but first in my heart: thank you, Dear Husband, for being awesome. I love you!

CHAPTER ONE

Georgia Hearn sat at the corner table in the sandwich shop and sipped her Diet Pepsi. She had refilled the damn thing so many times she was amazed that they hadn't kicked her out yet. Making use of the free wi-fi, she stared at her laptop as if it might give her the answer to her prayers. Well, it might, right?

She typed "make money fast" into her search bar and sighed. She probably typed that in at least once a week. All it ever got her was a bunch of scams, several of which she had gamely fallen for. Getting paid to fill out surveys? Check. Run an easy, no-work-involved online store? Check. Stuffing envelopes at home? Assembling crafts? Double check. Or in her case, no check. No money.

Georgia closed her laptop, put her head in her hands and let her blonde hair fall over her face. What was the point? She was broke. Wishing that weren't the case wasn't going to help her situation. She needed money—now. She'd been buying groceries on her credit card and that was now officially maxed out. Forget paying rent this month. She shouldn't even have agreed to meet her girlfriend Casey for lunch, not when she knew she'd have to pretend she just ate so Casey wouldn't feel bad for her.

"Georgia?"

Georgia pulled her head out of her hands and jumped up to see Casey smiling at her.

"Hey there!" Georgia gave Casey a quick hug and sat back down. "Go order your lunch, I was starving so I already ate," she lied.

Casey rolled her eyes. "Little Miss Manners? I doubt it. Don't worry about it, lunch is on me."

Georgia laughed. Casey knew her way too well sometimes. They had been friends since high school and even now that they were both twenty-two and didn't see each other all the time anymore, Casey still knew the way Georgia's brain worked.

"Casey, I can't take your money."

Casey pulled out her wallet and quickly flashed it Georgia's way. Holy shit. The girl had cash. Lots of it.

"Yeah, you can," Casey said.

"What the hell are you into, Case?"

Casey laughed and bought them sandwiches before coming back and sitting across from Georgia. "This is nothing. I made five hundred bucks last night in two hours."

"No way."

"Yes way. I can get you a gig too, you know."

Georgia's stomach fluttered at the idea of having five hundred bucks in two hours. She started doing the math in her head. If she could do whatever Casey had done every day of the week, she'd have $10,000 in a month, and in a year she'd be pulling in six figures.

"Are you stripping again? Because you know I have the rhythm of someone having an epileptic fit."

"No dancing." Casey sipped her soda primly and grinned.

"So what did you do?" Georgia looked at the devilish glint in her friend's eyes and gasped. "Tell me you are not...an escort!"

"I am not an escort. I work at a club."

"Doing what?" Georgia took a bite of the sandwich Casey handed her. *Delicious.*

"It's a gentleman's club for men who like things not so gentle, if you catch my drift."

"Uh, no, actually I don't. What are you talking about?"

Casey laughed. "I get paid to play with them and to let them play with me. Sometimes I put on a show where I'll get spanked or whipped in front of them, and if they like what they see I get tipped very, very well. The more stuff I do, the more money I make."

Georgia's mouth dropped open. "What did you do last night to make five hundred dollars?"

Casey finished the food that was in her mouth before responding. "I rode the wooden pony for an hour."

"And the second hour?"

"I just lay on my back with my legs tied open so they could all see my bruised pussy and they walked by me and put money on my belly. Twenties and fifties, even."

Georgia nodded. She was used to Casey's outrageous stories. The girl was not shy, that was for sure. "Wow. So what's that mean, you rode the wooden pony?"

Casey laughed. "It was awful. I'm so sore, that's why I need you to cover for me tonight."

"Cover for you? Tonight? Wait, why are you sore?" If it was so awful, why was Casey laughing?

"Imagine straddling a bar in such a way that all your weight falls on your pussy and you can only reposition yourself a little bit each time you go up on your tippy toes and come back down on your pussy again. Up and down, up and down, that's the ride. It starts getting pretty painful, so the longer I stay on the more money I make."

Georgia laughed. "You got paid just to sit there for an hour?"

"Hey, it wasn't like I didn't earn it. Just try it yourself, you'll see."

"Gladly. I could use some easy money," Georgia said.

"Tonight you won't have to do anything that difficult.

They don't usually put on the same show two nights in a row. I'm just so sore I really need a night off. So will you really do it? You'll cover for me?"

"Absolutely." Georgia smiled at her friend. Things were looking up.

* * * * *

Georgia tugged at the short black leather skirt she had borrowed from Casey's closet and went up to the large man standing outside the very ordinary-looking storefront. *Must be the bouncer.* But this place didn't look like any of the clubs she'd ever been to. It seemed so...sedate. After the bouncer looked her up and down, he wordlessly opened the large door and stepped aside.

No loud pulsating music blasted out of the club. There was some music, but it was soft, like the ambient stuff they played in elevators in fancy hotels. She walked into a lounge-type area where a bunch of men in expensive suits were sitting around on couches and recliners. Some were smoking cigars. She walked past them, past the bar and the bartender to the back room, just like Casey told her to do. She knocked.

The door swung open and an attractive woman in her forties smiled and gestured for her to come into the office. It looked like Georgia always imagined a hotshot lawyer's office would look. Leather chairs, lots of mahogany, that sort of thing.

"I'm Mary Ann," the woman said as she shook Georgia's hand. "You must be Casey's friend."

"Yes ma'am," Georgia said. "Nice to meet you."

Mary Ann sat down in one of the big leather chairs and said, "Casey said you've never worked at an establishment like GC."

"GC?"

"Gentlemen's Club, of course," Mary Ann said. "We call it GC."

"Oh." Georgia smiled nervously. "I may not have experience, but I'm a very hard worker, ma'am."

"You don't need to call me ma'am. Mary Ann will do just fine. Tonight we have a very simple, interactive performance for our clients. I'll be very straight with you and if you're not interested, now's the time to let me know."

"Okay. Mary Ann."

"All you have to do is lie on a platform with your legs tied open and let our clients perform cunnilingus on you."

"Cunnilingus?"

"Oral sex."

"Oh, you mean they're going to eat me out?" Georgia raised her eyebrows. That didn't seem like a performance really. "What's the performance part of it?"

"That's it. The other clients like to watch a pretty young woman being pleasured. It's all very sanitary, if that's what you're worried about. We keep a roll of plastic wrap next to you and each gentleman is required to use a fresh piece and keep that barrier between you and his mouth."

Plastic wrap instead of nice, warm tongue? "Eww." Georgia winced when she realized she'd said that aloud.

Mary Ann laughed. "You won't even feel that it's there. We pay you one hundred dollars for an hour of this, and whatever tips you earn on top of that are yours to keep. You can expect each gentleman to tip between ten and twenty dollars after he's had his turn with you. Of course they are not required to tip anyone but they are, after all, gentlemen."

"So I gather." Georgia smiled. "I'm in."

Mary Ann handed her a single typed piece of paper. "Just sign this and give me your driver's license to photocopy for our records."

Georgia signed the paper and dug into her little purse for her ID.

A man walked into the office and gave Mary Ann a kiss on the cheek before turning to Georgia and nodding. "So this is Casey's friend Georgia, I gather."

Georgia nodded and put her hand out to the man. "Hello, sir."

"I'm Vincent, Mary Ann's husband. We run GC. Geez, you look like a teenager." He turned to his wife. "Did you check her ID?" When Mary Ann nodded, Vincent turned his attention back to Georgia. "Are you ready?"

"Yes." Georgia hoped she sounded more confident than she felt. "What do I do?"

"Just follow me." Vincent walked back out the office door and Georgia did as he said and followed him to a different part of the club. There was a stage and a bunch of tables, like a dinner theater setup. On the stage was a chair.

"You sit there, in that chair. When the gentlemen come in for the show, I'll tell you to take off your clothes and you'll strip onstage."

"I-I'm not a stripper. I mean, I can't dance or anything."

"That's fine, pretend you're at home taking your clothes off for a lover. Just strip. Then I'll ask you to sit down and I'll get a volunteer from the audience to tie you up. You just have to follow directions. If at any point you are uncomfortable, say 'umbrella' and I'll untie you and send you home. Of course, you wouldn't have kept your half of the contract in that case, so you would forfeit your salary at that point."

"Okay."

"What's the safeword? Say it."

"Umbrella."

"Good girl. Now just sit there and wait for a few minutes," Vincent said. "We'll be ready to start soon."

* * * * *

Georgia sat on the chair trying to look out at the audience, but the spotlight on her practically blinded her. She could hear the men though, talking in deep voices, the ice clinking in their drinks, an occasional burst of laughter. She could smell cigar smoke. She thought smoking inside had been banned—apparently some laws didn't apply here at GC.

Vincent came onstage next to her and grabbed a microphone. "Gentlemen, your attention please."

Silence fell over the club. Georgia didn't know what to do, she was so nervous. One hundred dollars for one hour. That's what she needed to focus on. A hundred bucks plus tips. She smiled out at the audience even though she couldn't see them past the bright spotlight.

Vincent came up behind her and put one large hand on her shoulder as he held the microphone in the other hand. "It is my pleasure to introduce the lovely Georgia to the Gentlemen's Club. Sweet Georgia, please show these fine men that gorgeous body you have under all those clothes!"

He stepped aside and gave her a *go on now* look.

Georgia stood on shaky knees and slowly pulled her low-cut V-neck blouse over her head, revealing her lacy black push-up bra. The men cheered and whistled. She blushed and grinned. No wonder Casey got off on stripping. She'd never had a man actually yell in delight and whistle when she undressed before.

She reached around behind her waist and unzipped the miniskirt she had borrowed from Casey. It was leather and it was tight, so she had to shimmy a bit to lower and then step out of it. The men actually started clapping.

"Thank you, you're so kind," she said, laughing.

Vincent chuckled and spoke into the mic as she stood on the stage wearing nothing but her high heels, a black thong and her push-up bra. "Can I get a volunteer to cuff Sweet Georgia to the chair, gentlemen?"

She didn't know how Vincent could see past the spotlight that was so blinding to her, but maybe he was just used to it. He pointed to someone sitting at one of the tables. "Jonathan Syler, I do believe it's your turn, sir."

Everyone clapped, which she assumed meant that Jonathan Syler had left his table to join them onstage. She couldn't make out anything happening in the audience, but then the man came around to the side of the stage. The lighting hid his face, but she could see his form. He was huge—six foot three at least, with shoulders like a football player. Georgia watched with interest as he stepped up the stairs. He was wearing an expensive-looking suit. Maybe he'd just gotten off work and swung by the club on his way home?

When the man stood next to her, she had to crane her neck up to look at him properly. He was gorgeous! He didn't smile at her though, which was a bit disconcerting, just looked at her with deep brown eyes and carefully took off his jacket. Vincent took it from him, holding it folded over his arm.

"Take off your bra," the man said. His voice was low, commanding. How old was he? Thirties, maybe? He didn't look like any of the frat boys Georgia had dated in the past, that was for sure. He looked like…a man. Georgia felt a frisson of awareness in her body as she slowly followed his direction. He nodded his approval when she dropped the bra on the floor of the stage.

The men in the audience cheered.

"Very nice, Georgia," he said. He was talking quietly, for only her to hear. "Now take off your panties."

Georgia hooked her thumbs under the sides of her thong and drew it down to her ankles, where she carefully stepped out of the panties without taking off her high heels. Suddenly Georgia was very aware of the fact that she was standing there completely naked on a stage in a room full of men. The testosterone in the air was so thick she could practically taste it.

Her hands were shaking. Why was she scared now? The exit wasn't more than a few yards away. She could be out of there in a moment if she wanted. And she could always say "umbrella". She forced herself to take in a long, slow breath and looked him in the eyes.

He smiled then. His whole demeanor changed with that smile. Georgia was so happy to have made him smile that the room of men seemed to melt away, as if it were just her and Jonathan, alone on the stage.

"Lovely," Jonathan said softly. In a louder voice he said, "Please, sit."

She sat.

"Spread your legs, Georgia."

A hundred dollars, she thought. One hundred. Georgia spread her legs, opening her knees without shame. If she thought too hard about what she was doing she would have a heart attack. She just had to stop thinking and enjoy herself. This was the easiest money she'd ever had the opportunity to make—and she had to admit having all of those men watch her was a huge turn-on.

Jonathan knelt in front of her and held his hand out to Vincent, who handed him several leather cuffs. Georgia looked down at the chair with renewed interest—it was a bondage chair. It had places for cuffs to hook on and everything. She had played with light bondage before with past boyfriends and enjoyed it. Just having her hands tied with a scarf, really. None of the guys she had dated really had a lot of experience with that type of thing though.

Jonathan took her ankle in his hand and caressed it gently as he wrapped one of the wide leather cuffs around it, attaching the cuff to one leg of the chair. Georgia felt a rush of wetness in her core as he opened her legs even wider than they were already spread to cuff her other ankle to the opposite leg of the chair.

She fought the urge to cover her exposed pussy with her hands.

Jonathan took both of her hands in his larger ones and held them. Looking at her face thoughtfully, he winked as he kissed her hand as if she were royalty or something—and then he stood and cuffed her wrists behind her back.

"Are you comfortable?" he asked.

Georgia thought about it, feeling her position, spread and tied to the chair. "Yes," she said. "Thank you."

He held a sash in front of her and looked at her again

as if he were trying to read her thoughts. "I'm going to blindfold you. Then I'm going to lick your pussy for a few minutes before I let the other gentlemen have their turn. But I'll be back at the end to free you from your bonds."

She nodded. This was crazy. Thank goodness for the blindfold, because if she had to watch all of those men staring at her as she got her pussy eaten she'd freak out. No, no she wouldn't. Who was she kidding, anyway? She was wet already just at the thought of it.

Jonathan tied the blindfold around her head tightly.

The world went dark and her other senses sharpened. She could hear a tearing sound. What was that? Oh right. The plastic wrap. She felt Jonathan's large warm hands as he took two fingers and slowly spread her labia until her clit was fully exposed, and only then did he put the thin piece of clear plastic over her pussy. Man, that felt weird.

Then his mouth was *on her*...he slowly licked up the center of her nether lips, causing tingles all the way to her toes. She inhaled sharply as he made circles with his tongue.

His warm breath tickled her pussy as he spoke, his voice quiet enough that she could tell his words were meant for her ears only.

"Sweet Georgia," he whispered, and her name on his lips made her flush with heat. "I have a question for you."

She nodded silently, not sure if he was even looking at her face since she couldn't see anything.

He took a moment to reply, pausing to lick her clit with lazy circles. "How do you feel about...chastity belts?"

How did he know? she wondered. How could this man—this stranger—possibly know? Being locked in a chastity belt was one of her go-to fantasies. She laughed uncomfortably.

"I'm guessing Casey told you about the story I found online," she murmured, embarrassed.

"Tell me the story," he said, and sucked her clit into his mouth, plastic wrap intact. She gasped, but just the thought of the story was getting her even more turned-on than Jonathan's perfect technique.

"There was a girl," she started, sure she was blushing, "and her master made her wear a chastity belt for an entire week. He wouldn't let her come—he just teased her until she thought she'd die." She felt on the brink of orgasm just from the memory of reading that story on a fetish site.

"What would you do," he asked slowly, "if I put a chastity belt on you, and wouldn't take it off for a week?"

She moaned. This couldn't really be happening. How on earth did Jonathan know her most secret fantasy—how did he know that just talking to her about the idea made her ready to come?

"If you put a chastity belt on me," she breathed, "I'd be yours, all locked up, just for you—until you set me free."

She was right there on the edge of climaxing, her pussy clamping, wishing she had Jonathan's cock inside her—this stranger who seemed to know her most inner self. He knew exactly what he was doing.

Don't stop, don't stop, she thought, but then his tongue was gone and she felt the plastic being pulled away from her pussy.

She heard Jonathan's voice as he stepped aside and another man came forward. "She's delightful," he said. "Enjoy."

* * * * *

Jonathan went back to his table and picked up his scotch on the rocks; the ice was melting and watering down the liquor. He let the scotch slide down his throat and smiled. Sweet Georgia was very sweet indeed. He watched her as she sat, bound to the chair by the cuffs he had put on her, her head tilted back and her pretty mouth slightly open as if in ecstasy while yet another man buried his face between her legs.

She moaned loudly and her legs shook and Jonathan could feel his erection threatening to burst out of his slacks. He'd been a member of GC for three years now.

He'd always enjoyed the entertainment. But this girl—this girl evoked a visceral response in him unlike anything he'd ever felt before.

He had to have her.

He hadn't expected Georgia to respond to his inquiry about the chastity belt with such ferocious passion. The image of Georgia's tender pussy locked up from anyone but him made him shift in his seat, his hard cock becoming almost painful.

He imagined dragging her, still bound to the chair, behind the curtain. He would take that blindfold off her so that she could see exactly who he was, but he'd use the sash to gag her gorgeous mouth so she couldn't make a sound. Then he'd drop his pants and fuck her right there as she stared into his eyes like she had onstage when he told her to strip off her bra and panties.

Not that he would actually want to rape her. It wouldn't be the gentlemanly thing to do…unless she gave him permission ahead of time. He needed her to want him as much as he wanted her. Would she be the type of girl who'd let him take her like that? She could be. She was here, after all.

He had to see her again. There was no way he was going to let her walk away after this night was over if there was a possibility she'd never come back. He had to figure out a way to ensure she'd return…

Another man was licking her cunt and, judging by the frantic tossing of her head as she grunted and moaned, she was starting to get a little overstimulated from all those tongues. Good. That was how he liked it. He laughed and took another sip of his scotch as he settled back in his seat to watch the show.

She still had another forty minutes of forced orgasms before he'd uncuff her.

CHAPTER TWO

Georgia cried out as she had her seventh orgasm of the evening. These men were merciless, torturing her swollen clit with their tongues, each man coming to her with new energy and vigor as he licked her pussy with his own signature style. One man spent his turn gently nibbling her little nub with his teeth, causing her to strain in her bonds and try to escape even as she came all over herself.

With the blindfold on, she had no idea how long she'd been there or how much longer she would be enduring the talented tongues of the Gentlemen's Club clientele. Then she heard a familiar voice.

Jonathan.

Her pulse inexplicably raced at the sound of his voice as he leaned into her ear. She could feel the warmth of his skin, feel the whisper of his hot breath on her ear and smell just the slightest whiff of expensive cologne.

"Have you had enough, Georgia?"

Georgia didn't know what to say. She instinctively tried to close her legs, forgetting again that they were bound far apart.

She felt his hand drop between her thighs and she moaned as he dipped his finger deep inside her pussy—

and there was definitely no plastic wrap there. His finger felt so good and so wrong at the same time. She shouldn't be letting him do this. How could she want Jonathan so much when she had just been thoroughly sated by a dozen other men?

Of course. It was all that talk about the chastity belt. Casey had to have been behind that—she must have tutored Jonathan on exactly what to say to have Georgia begging for more. That had to be it. Right?

She heard the other men in the audience start cheering and clapping. What on earth were they going on about now?

Then she felt it.

Something smooth and cold as ice was being slid under her buttocks. It felt like a thin piece of metal nestled against her ass crack. The same metal, but wider it seemed, pressed against her pussy and then Jonathan's hands firmly gripped her waist. She heard a... a *click*.

The applause grew louder. What on earth? She fought the urge to say "umbrella" and get the hell out of there. She wouldn't, not now.

The blindfold came off. Georgia squinted at the bright spotlight until her eyes readjusted. Jonathan smiled and knelt before her, dropping a tender kiss to her inner thigh in a quick, almost secretive motion before he uncuffed first one ankle and then the other. She looked down—what had he placed on her?

She gasped. It couldn't be. Georgia didn't say a word until Jonathan uncuffed her wrists. The she immediately grabbed at what looked like a stainless steel thong between her legs. It was literally locked into place.

No way. She had to be dreaming. Fantasizing still. Because if this was actually happening, then she was in way over her head.

"Get this off of me!" she said, struggling to keep her voice calm.

Jonathan grinned. "Of course, it's just part of the

14

show," he whispered. "The men just like to see it, that's all. Now pick up your money and blow a kiss to your fans."

Her money? *Oh that's right!* She looked on the ground below the chair and saw it was covered in ten- and twenty-dollar bills. She grinned and picked them up quickly, trying to look as sexy and graceful as possible while crawling around under the chair on her knees. She couldn't count it just yet, she'd have to wait until later. After Jonathan unlocked the chastity belt.

Georgia picked her rumpled clothing off the floor before she stood and did as Jonathan said, smiling and blowing kisses to the audience. She walked off the stage, naked except for the metal device locked around her groin, and sauntered into the back office. The cash sure felt nice crumpled in her hand.

She looked over her shoulder. Good. Jonathan was following her with the key. She knocked on the office door and when she didn't hear an answer she stepped inside. Jonathan stepped into the office and closed the door quietly behind him.

"You did great," he said.

My goodness, he's a handsome devil. Georgia smiled and turned to put her bra on.

"I've seen you naked," he said, amusement creeping into his deep voice. "Why would you turn around so I can't see your breasts as you dress?"

Georgia laughed and turned around again. "I don't know. Can you unlock me so I can put my panties and skirt back on?"

"You can put your skirt back on over the chastity belt."

The thought stopped her cold. Her fantasy was just that, a fantasy. She could never act it out in real life, even if the thought turned her on. It just wasn't rational.

"Um, no thanks. I'm leaving now, so…unlock me."

Jonathan fingered the key in his hand before slipping it into his pocket. "No."

What does he mean, no?

Her pussy clenched in excitement at his refusal, but she shook her head. It had been fun to talk about, but this wasn't actually going to happen. She was done. She was taking her money and going home. Georgia quickly counted through the cash in her hand. Whoa. Two hundred dollars. That plus the one hundred from Vincent and Mary Ann and she had just made three hundred dollars in an hour.

She looked up at Jonathan and sighed. "Umbrella, then. I'm ready to call it a night."

"And I said no. I will not unlock your chastity belt." Jonathan's handsome face was serious and thoughtful.

"Didn't you hear me? I said the safeword. I said 'umbrella', that means I'm serious and you have to unlock me."

Jonathan took a step toward her and she had to tilt her chin up to gaze into his deep brown eyes. "I'm not playing a game anymore, Georgia. You're mine now. The chastity belt stays—for a full week, just like you told me."

His lips came down on hers then, pressing against her mouth until she felt herself melting into his kiss, opening her mouth to receive his tongue despite her best intentions not to encourage him.

"Please," she whispered. "Unlock me."

But even as the words came out of her mouth, she knew that if he did unlock her, she'd be disappointed. This man—this stranger—was making her fantasy come true.

"I will. Tomorrow. I'll meet you here at the club."

Tomorrow? She couldn't have this thing on her all night and day. Certainly not for a week, like he'd suggested earlier. Was he going to make her wear it again and again, until the week was up? She gasped, amazed that even after having been so thoroughly satiated by the gentlemen at the club, she was still turned-on.

"What if I have to pee?" she asked lamely.

"There's little holes, see?" he said. "You just won't be able to have sex or masturbate, that's all."

"It's uncomfortable," she said. It actually wasn't uncomfortable at all, somehow.

"Too bad."

"I'll go to the police," she lied. Her ex-boyfriend was on the job, so there was no way she could go down to the precinct and tell them what had happened.

"Go then. Tell them all about it," Jonathan said with a grin.

Damn him. How could he be so sure she wasn't really going to go to the cops? He didn't know about her ex. But he did know that she didn't really want him to unlock her—because he had tricked her into giving her implicit permission.

Georgia let out a growl of frustration as she pulled her miniskirt up over the chastity belt.

"I'll see you here tomorrow night," Jonathan said.

Georgia stormed past him and walked out the office door, nearly running into Vincent on her way out. "Vincent," she said. "Your client put a chastity belt on me."

To her surprise, Vincent just laughed. "He really did it, huh?"

"What? Make him take it *off.*"

Vincent handed her five twenty-dollar bills. "Don't worry about him, he's a good guy. You put on quite the show, Sweet Georgia. Come back anytime."

"Did you not hear me?" she asked, not even caring at this point if he thought she was rude. "Jonathan Syler has put a chastity belt on me and locked it and he won't *un*lock it."

Vincent's brow furrowed. "I'll make him take it off you if that's what you really want."

Georgia paused. "No," she whispered, her cheeks getting hot. "That's okay. I can handle him."

Vincent laughed again and shook his head. "He always warned me he was going to do that—once he found the right girl."

Georgia's mouth dropped open in shock.

"I thought he was kidding," Vincent continued, "since he's been a client of GC for three years and has yet to find any woman he considered worthy enough to wear his chastity belt."

"Are you fucking serious?" Georgia scowled. Jonathan chose that moment to step out of the office and waved as he passed by her on his way to the lounge.

"See you tomorrow, Georgia," he said, and he winked, patting the pocket he'd slipped the key into.

This was ridiculous. He was actually going to do this— to make her go home wearing the chastity belt. In all of her fantasies, she had never really thought about the fact that being locked up meant just that—and she had no control over it. Moisture pooled between her legs and she bit back a smile. Even though she was miffed, she was way too tired to fight.

Fuck it. Georgia sighed. "Tomorrow then."

* * * * *

Georgia woke up the following morning and looked over at the digital clock on her bedside table. Okay, afternoon. There was a moment of blissful amnesia where she forgot all about the night before, but it didn't last long. She looked down at her waist. It was still there.

How on earth had she gotten herself into this situation? She really couldn't go to the police. What was she supposed to do, walk right up to her ex and tell him that a tall, dark and handsome stranger had randomly decided that she was the woman who should wear his chastity belt? How could she tell him, or any of her ex-boyfriend's cop cronies, exactly what she'd been doing when said stranger had locked up her pussy? Could she admit to them that before he put the chastity belt on her she had told him she thought the whole idea was totally hot?

She started laughing. *Laugh or cry*, she mused. And this was fucking hysterical. She stared closely at the lock that closed the metal band around her hips. Okay. She had seen people pick locks like this before, on TV at least. She got up and walked naked, except for the chastity belt, to her dresser top. A moment later she stood leaning against the dresser with a bobby pin in her hand, attempting to pick the lock.

Who was she kidding? She was no lock-picking burglar type. And now she had a more pressing problem. She had to pee.

Georgia quickly rubbed body lotion over her thighs and hips and tried halfheartedly to push the belt down her legs. That didn't work, but she hadn't expected it to anyway.

There were little holes all through the bottom of the belt that ran over her nether lips. She supposed that was a good thing, it would let her pee and also let air in. But how was she supposed to wipe? Georgia could scream in frustration. She never thought about the whole bathroom situation when she'd fantasized about chastity belts before.

Fuck it. She went into the bathroom and sat over the toilet, watching in amusement as she peed through the damned chastity belt. Disgusting. How was this supposed to be a turn-on?

When she went back to GC tonight she was going to wait until Jonathan had unlocked her and then she was going to smack him silly. Why would a man that gorgeous need to get a woman to see him again in such a forcible manner? Because he was crazy as…as a man who would put a chastity belt on a woman.

They must be a good match, because she was crazy enough to let him. She sighed. Unbelievable.

Her cell phone rang and she picked it up and hit "answer" even though she didn't recognize the number.

"Good morning, Georgia." It was Jonathan—she'd recognize that deep baritone anywhere, especially after he had spoken to her while she was blindfolded.

"Good morning to you, you sick son of a bitch," she said pleasantly.

"I hope your evening wasn't ruined by the chastity

belt," he said.

"I had to pee with it on," she said tonelessly.

"That's fine, don't worry about it. I'm mainly concerned that you understand why you're wearing it."

Georgia sat back on her bed and sighed. Probably because she had told him that if he put one on her she'd like it. But there was no way she was going to admit that. "Because you're a nutcase?"

Jonathan laughed and for some reason, she smiled. "Perhaps," he said. "I wanted to make sure I'd get to see you again. And in the meantime, I want to make sure that you don't have sex with anyone else and that you don't masturbate."

"Why would you care if I masturbated?"

"Because I want control over your orgasms. I loved watching you last night, your legs tied open with one man after another licking your pussy until you couldn't take it anymore—and then watching you as they just kept on going. It turned me on."

Georgia felt her pulse race at the mention of last night's "performance" at the club. It had turned her on too. But hearing Jonathan talk about it was somehow even more of a turn-on. That voice of his... She could feel her pussy getting wet and she dropped her hand between her legs without even thinking about it.

And met with cold, hard stainless steel.

"Georgia," he said. She pressed the phone closer to her ear as if that would bring him closer to her. "Tonight, I want to whip you onstage for the gentlemen. Will you allow me the honor?"

She had never been properly whipped before. Sure, she had played a bit with past boyfriends, but none of them even owned an actual whip, and if they did they certainly didn't know how to wield it for her sexual pleasure. But to be whipped as part of a performance—should she do it?

"Yes," she said. "But I want you to come over right now and take this chastity belt off of me."

Would he do it? If he did, she wondered if he'd make her go back in it. Locked up for the full week... As terrifying as the idea was, she couldn't help but admit to herself the idea excited her. Jonathan laughed again and she nearly threw the phone across the room. It was as if he could read her mind.

"I don't think so," he said. "But how about this—you can come to me."

Georgia sat up quickly. "Where are you?"

"At my apartment." He gave her the address. "I'll see you in an hour."

"And then you'll take this thing off of me, right?"

"Um, no."

* * * * *

Georgia took the subway to the Upper West Side and double-checked Jonathan's address before she walked through the subway exit.

What does he do for a living, anyway, to afford a place in this neighborhood?

His building even had a doorman. Georgia looked down at her simple sundress—the only outfit that would definitely cover up the fact she was wearing metal underwear—and sighed. She wished she could have spent the three hundred bucks she earned last night on a new wardrobe instead of bills and groceries. *C'est la vie.*

She got onto the elevator and almost laughed when she realized she was going up to the penthouse. *Really, Mr. Jonathan Syler? Really?*

The elevator opened directly into his foyer. And there he was, wearing designer jeans and a simple T-shirt that probably cost him a hundred dollars, looking devastatingly handsome and so annoying Georgia wanted to smack him.

"Nice place," she said. She couldn't keep the surprise out of her voice.

"Thanks." He leaned in and kissed her cheek as if she didn't despise him. "It's good to see you again."

Georgia laughed. "I'm only here for one reason. Get

this thing off of me before I go to the police." *That's good*, she thought. *Almost sounds as if I mean it.*

"Sure," he said. "Let's go in the bedroom, away from the windows." She looked around at the large living room. *Wow*. Windows encased the entire room, offering an incredible view.

Georgia followed him, her gaze straying to the delectable ass hidden under those expensive jeans.

The bedroom had windows as well, but they were covered in drapes that hung to the plush carpet beneath her feet. There was a four-poster bed in the center of the room. Georgia looked at the bed and smiled. She could just picture all sorts of fun games they could play on a bed like that.

Focus, woman! Just get him to unlock you and get out of here. Ugh. Who was she kidding? She hadn't been this turned-on since...well, ever.

Jonathan came up behind her and wrapped his arms around her. He dipped his head to her neck. Goose bumps covered her flesh as he licked her skin there for just a second before planting a little kiss under her earlobe.

"Jonathan," she said, trying to scold him.

He turned her around in his arms and kissed her lips, effectively silencing her. He tasted good—like toothpaste and an underlying taste of man. A bit salty.

She surprised herself by opening her lips to him, letting his tongue invade her mouth and then kissing him back with a ferocity that had her wondering just why she was so angry with him to begin with. She felt a tingle in her pussy as his hand caressed her breast over the thin cotton sundress she wore and she pressed her mound to his thigh, expecting to feel delicious pressure and instead felt...nothing. The metal chastity belt was keeping her from contact.

"Get this thing off of me," she growled, dipping her tongue into his mouth, fully expecting him to unlock her immediately so that they could consummate their time together.

She pulled the cotton sundress over her shoulders and tossed it into a heap on the carpet and stood before him, naked except for the chastity belt. She thrust a hip in his direction, the unspoken plea on her lips. *Unlock me, unlock me.*

Jonathan pulled his T-shirt over his head and threw it onto the floor as well. She ran her fingers down his well-muscled chest. A scattering of dark crinkly hairs led a trail down below his belt and she let her fingers linger there, caressing the hair. He put his hand on her breast then, cupping it carefully before bringing his thumb up to her nipple, flicking it into hard erection.

With her nipples tight and sticking out like little pencil erasers, he brought his hot mouth down over one and nibbled it continuously until she was moaning with desire. She could feel herself getting wetter and wetter as he twisted her other nipple, pulling and playing with her until she wanted nothing more than to get as close to him as physically possible.

She wanted to ride him. She wanted to be ridden.

"Fuck me, Jonathan, please, please," she moaned as he continued to tease her nipples, stringing a bright invisible line of pleasure directly between her breasts and her clit. He was like a musician, plucking and plucking that string for all it was worth.

"No," he breathed, dipping his head to her breast and licking her once more. "No."

She cried out in frustration and pushed his face away from her trembling body. "Damn it, Jonathan! Unlock me so we can finish what you started!"

He just smiled and shook his head. "You don't really want me to unlock you, now do you."

It wasn't a question—but Georgia knew the answer must be written all over her face. As much as she wanted him and wanted out of the chastity belt, she'd be disappointed if he really did let her go so easily. She had told him if he locked her up, she'd be his. And now she was.

"Tonight, Sweet Georgia. I'll unlock you tonight, at the club."

"Do you promise?"

Jonathan came up to her and held her chin, forcing her to look directly into his chocolate-colored eyes. "You must promise me something. If I unlock you, will you let me whip your pretty little pussy?"

Georgia nodded. She'd never had her pussy whipped before, but she had always liked the sound of it. It sounded dark and fun and erotic. She'd never trusted any of her previous boyfriends to know what they were doing enough to let them come near her most sensitive area with anything so potentially damaging as a whip. But Jonathan…Jonathan obviously knew what he was doing. She trusted him, although heaven knew why she did.

"I'm getting hard right now," he murmured, "just thinking of your legs tied open, taking my whip on your little clit with the entire Gentlemen's Club in attendance to see the beautiful woman I've chosen to wear my chastity belt."

Georgia swallowed hard at the idea of doing something so personal and intimate and potentially frightening onstage in front of an audience. But even an offer to fuck him right then and there wasn't getting him to unlock her chastity belt. Agreeing to this performance might just be the only way to ensure he'd unlock her, even if just for a short time.

Well, that—and there was the fact that she was completely intrigued by the whole notion.

"Okay," Georgia agreed. "I'll do it. Will it hurt?"

Jonathan took her hand in his and rested it on the bulging cock trapped beneath his jeans. "Yes," he said.

Georgia laughed and unzipped his jeans slowly, asking with her eyes if she could play with him.

"Yes," he answered the unspoken question.

She tugged his jeans down his hips and his cock practically sprang out, lying thick and hard in her hand, the head almost purple it was so hard. The tip glistened with a pearl of pre-cum. Licking her lips, she dropped to her knees in front of him. She looked up at him, imploring him with her eyes, *May I?*

"Oh Georgia," he groaned.

She parted her lips and took his cock into her mouth, swallowing the length of him, wrapping her palm around the base, weighing his heavy testicles in her hand and feeling the vulnerability of him there. She literally had him by the balls. She flicked her tongue up and down the underside of his cock, loving the feel of it twitching in her mouth as he stood above her.

She caressed his balls firmly, letting one finger stray to the little area between his asshole and his balls and pressed lightly, tapping the taint a bit as he groaned in satisfaction.

Suddenly she pulled her mouth off him. "Unlock the belt," she commanded.

Jonathan looked down at her in surprise and grabbed her hair. "I told you already what will happen. Tonight before I whip your pussy I'll unlock you, but not a moment before."

"Then I won't finish you off," she threatened with a smile.

Jonathan smiled but it looked more like a threat—or a promise. "Open your mouth," he said in a low, commanding voice.

Georgia demurred, shaking her head with her lips tightly pursed. Jonathan sighed, reached his hand down and held her nostrils shut with his fingers.

"Hey—" Georgia sputtered in surprise.

Jonathan grinned down at her. "Now that your mouth is open, would you kindly continue?"

Georgia couldn't help but laugh. *The man has balls, that's for sure.* She nodded, making his fingers slip off her nose, and proffered her mouth to his length.

"Thank god," he said as he thrust his cock back into her mouth, holding her by her hair, taking control of her head as he moved her physically up and down his length.

Georgia would have bitten him if she weren't so desperate to taste his semen down the back of her throat. She couldn't help it...once she got started tasting a cock that yummy she just had to see it through to the end. But how could he possibly have known that?

He came then, a hot jet pouring down her throat. "Swallow me," he said.

She did, relishing the feel of him in her mouth, bruising her lips with his thrusts. When he finally let her hair go she practically fell back onto the carpet.

He looked down at her and offered one well-muscled arm to help her stand. "The next time you pull a stunt like that, your punishment will be much worse than that," he informed her.

Georgia felt herself get wet again but she refused to think about it. It wasn't fair, him getting to come while she was denied her release.

"Please, please make me come," she begged.

"I'll see you tonight," he said. He picked her sundress off the floor and dressed her as if she were a doll. "Vincent pays well for girls to get pussy-whipped."

Georgia was already walking back to the front foyer when he said that. She turned around in surprise. "You mean I'm going to get paid again?"

Jonathan laughed. "Not for this. But for tonight, yes, of course. You'll be putting on a show. Just show up a bit early and hammer out the details with Vincent and Mary Ann."

Georgia smiled, her mood perking up instantly. She was going to make money doing something that she would happily have done for free.

Hell, she'd probably have paid for the experience, if she could have afforded it. And Jonathan was sticking to his guns, despite her demands to be freed—which made her desire him even more.

Things were certainly looking up.

CHAPTER THREE

Later that night, Casey and Georgia stood with Vincent and Mary Ann in their back office. Mary Ann had been suitably shocked and dismayed Jonathan Syler had put a chastity belt on Georgia and was refusing to remove it, but when she realized he would be taking it off that evening she looked relieved.

"I hope you had a talk with him, Vincent," Mary Ann said.

"Not exactly. Don't worry about it, Mary Ann," he said, laughing. "It's all in good fun, right, Georgia?"

Seeing as how he was paying her salary that evening, Georgia figured it wouldn't help to express her annoyance. Especially since the worst thing about wearing the darn thing was that she couldn't make herself come when she wanted to, which, after that stunt Jonathan pulled that afternoon at his penthouse, was making her very uncomfortable. Her pussy was swollen with unrequited need.

"Okay, here's the plan, Georgia. A couple minutes of stripping, and then you are going to be the one who ties up Miss Casey here for her spanking, which we will pay you twenty dollars to administer and Casey will get eighty dollars to take."

Casey grinned and squeezed Georgia's hand. Georgia blinked. She was going to spank her friend? *Weird.*

"Then," Vincent continued, "Casey will tie you up and hand you over to Mr. Jonathan Syler, who has requested the opportunity to be the first man to spank your pussy. You'll get one fifty for a few pussy slaps, and then you will stay tied open while the gentlemen pay their respects and give you tips for a job well done."

"One fifty?" Georgia asked.

"One hundred and fifty dollars—that's what we usually pay for a pussy spanking," Mary Ann said. "Don't worry, Mr. Syler knows what he's doing. He's studied with the best of them and he certainly has perfected his technique on the girls here in the past."

Why was Georgia suddenly feeling a little jealous of the girls Jonathan played with in the past? He could do whatever he wanted. What did she care?

"Oh hey," she said, "Jonathan mentioned he wanted to whip me. And whip my pussy."

Mary Ann raised her eyebrows. "Darling, I don't want you to overexert yourself. Are you sure you're up for it? Because if you're not, that's all right too."

Casey looked at her. "I could take the whipping instead, if you want. You know I love me some extra cash."

"Um, no thanks, Case," Georgia said. "I'm up for it."

"Okay then, you'll get an extra hundred added to your payment," Vincent said, jotting down a note on his pad.

Sweet.

Casey took Georgia's hand and started pulling her toward the stage. "Come on, I have to show you how to spank me," she said.

Georgia started to follow her but stopped short when she saw Jonathan already sitting on the stage. He looked even more handsome than she remembered from that afternoon. How did he do that—get more good-looking every time she looked at him?

He glanced over at her and Casey and stood. "Hi there," he said. "I thought you might like me to take off the chastity belt."

Georgia's mouth dropped open. She was expecting to have to fight with him about it—to threaten him, even. She nodded, hell yes she wanted the chastity belt off. So why was she just a bit disappointed? But it wasn't as if she was going to remind him that he told her he'd keep her locked up for a week. No way.

He smiled politely and ignored Casey, who was standing next to her and looking at him with interest. Jonathan dropped to his knees in front of Georgia and slid his hands up under her skirt.

"Hold your skirt up," he said.

Georgia did as she was told. She didn't care what Casey thought. They'd seen each other naked too many times while sharing clothing and whatnot for her to feel embarrassed in front of her friend.

Jonathan pulled the key out of his pocket and carefully unlocked the lock at the top of the chastity belt. The belt opened and Georgia could feel herself breathing a sigh of relief as the leather-lined stainless steel contraption fell to the floor with a clatter.

"Thank you," she said as she started to drop her skirt, but Jonathan stayed her hand with his.

"Not so fast," he murmured. He lifted her skirt back up and carefully touched and looked at her skin, checking every area the chastity belt had come into contact with. "No red marks, no abrasions. Good. You may go use the bathroom and clean up a bit, but I don't want you to masturbate. Do you agree?"

Georgia rolled her eyes. It wasn't his right to say whether or not she could masturbate. And after all the teasing he'd done that afternoon, if she didn't come soon she'd explode. She walked off to the bathroom without answering Jonathan.

She could hear Casey laughing behind her. "You are

gonna be so sorry, Georgie!" Georgia turned her head and looked at Casey but pointedly ignored Jonathan. She shrugged and kept walking.

In the bathroom Georgia used the facilities and then cleansed herself carefully, giving herself what Casey endearingly called "a whore's bath"—using the sink to wash just her armpits and her privates.

She leaned up against the tile wall and thought about Jonathan, teasing her so mercilessly that afternoon. Reaching down, she tapped her clit, remembering how much he had turned her on. The fact that he didn't want her to masturbate was just fuel for the fire. She rubbed harder, desperate for the release that had been forcibly denied her ever since that bastard had put the chastity belt on her. She came hard, not even bothering to stifle her cries. Finally satisfied, she washed her hands and walked out of the bathroom.

"I see you didn't listen to me," Jonathan said.

He had been standing right there this whole time? Georgia blushed.

"I tried to warn you."

"What do you mean?" she asked, annoyed and more than a little embarrassed at having been caught.

"Pussy-whipping hurts more when you've just come because your clit is swollen. There's more blood flow to the area. So you've just turned your experience from a little ouch to a positively masochistic ouch." Jonathan laughed and walked back toward the stage.

Georgia really disliked that man. It would be very helpful if he weren't so damn good-looking.

Casey's face lit up when she saw Georgia walking back onto the stage. The gentlemen had already started filtering in, bringing their drinks from the bar and talking amongst themselves. "Georgia!"

"So what am I supposed to be doing to you again?" Georgia asked.

Casey play growled and laughed. "You don't take this

very seriously, but just remember this place is like a fucking ATM. So you just use your hand, keep your wrist straight so you don't hurt yourself and spank my ass. I purposely keep my ass super pale when I tan so that it gets red very easily. Just stay away from the base of my spine and my hipbones so you don't actually hurt me."

Georgia nodded. "No problem."

"Just so you know, I like to make a lot of noise and complain a lot. That's the way to get good tips, if the guys think you really had to endure something."

"Good to know," Georgia murmured. She'd have to remember that for her pussy-whipping later.

Vincent came onstage with his handheld microphone and the men in the audience cheered. "Good evening, gentlemen! For your viewing pleasure, Sweet Georgia is here to spank Miss Casey for playing hooky last night!" The audience clapped.

Casey grabbed the mic and whined into it very dramatically, "I couldn't help it, my little pussy was so sore!"

The men cheered and she grinned, obviously not too sore to stop her performance. No, she seemed to be getting more and more into it.

"Now, Miss Casey," Vincent said sternly, "hold on to the back of that chair and bend over for Sweet Georgia."

"Noooo," Casey whined, looking as if she were trying not to smile as she said, "Please don't spank me too hard, Georgia!"

Wow, she plays the brat really, really well. The guys were eating it up.

Georgia stood to the side and looked at the bared white ass in front of her. Georgia lifted her hand and brought it down playfully, testing it out. Casey gasped and Georgia felt a thrill rush through her as she saw a little pink splotch on Casey's ass cheek from her hand. Her hand stung a bit, but she liked it.

Georgia wanted to say something to get the guys going,

but she had zero experience in showmanship. She'd just have to let Casey do her thing. But she could make her earn her eighty bucks in the meantime! Georgia brought her hand down again and again, relishing Casey's squeals and protests and the beautiful shade of pink her ass had become.

She was getting so into it that she didn't even notice that it was her turn until she saw Jonathan standing right over her.

"Casey," he said, stopping Georgia from continuing the spanking. "Do you want ten spanks from me on your ass, or just one spank on your pussy?"

Georgia laughed as she stepped aside. That had to be an easy choice. Ten was a lot more than one.

Face flushed, Casey looked over her shoulder and said, "Ten spanks on my ass, please."

Georgia's jaw dropped as she watched Jonathan pick Casey up and throw her over his knee while he sat in the very same chair she had just been holding on to. He counted off ten spanks and suddenly Georgia could hear the difference between the playing cries and squeals that Casey had given her and the real punishment that Jonathan was inflicting on her bottom.

If Casey was willing to endure this compared to just one spank on the pussy, then what had Georgia just signed herself up for?

Casey stood with Jonathan's help and rubbed her ass, frowning dramatically. She stepped off the stage and walked around the tables of men, smiling at them and letting them feel the heat radiating off her scorched buttocks. By the time Casey came back up onto the stage, she had ten-dollar bills stuffed all along her G-string and in her low-cut blouse.

"That was fun!" she said. "But you—you are so gonna earn your money, honey," she purred in Georgia's ear as she pushed Georgia into the chair and began cuffing her legs apart. The men cheered.

Georgia swallowed hard as Jonathan stood before her and looked down from his full height. He grinned. "Good thing your legs are tied apart, Sweet Georgia. Because there is no way in hell you'd keep them spread like that of your own volition...not after I get started."

She tried not to let her nervousness show in her face as she smiled gamely.

Jonathan slid his hand between her thighs and winced as she waited for the blow. But he didn't slap her pussy like she expected. Instead she felt him slowly rubbing her pussy lips with his palm in a deliberate circular motion. She closed her eyes and luxuriated in the moment—her back up against the hard wood chair, her legs so delightfully bound spread open, and the scent of Jonathan's cologne in the air as he leaned his head toward her and kissed her neck as if they were lovers alone in a room, not two virtual strangers performing on a stage.

She became slick and wet as her clit swelled under his gentle touch and then—*slap!* Georgia's eyes flew open and her knees tried to slam shut of their own accord as the sensation hit her hard. The gentlemen cheered as she looked up at Jonathan with her mouth open in shock.

"That was too hard, Jonathan!" she said. It would be better if he had a lighter touch, perhaps if he could just play with her pussy some more...

Jonathan laughed. "You really don't get a say in the matter, Sweet Georgia."

He slapped her pussy again so hard that she was sure it had to be in retaliation for her trying to tell him what to do. She couldn't keep the squeal from escaping her lips and embarrassingly her legs again struggled to close.

"You can either say the safeword and leave now," he said, "or you can take what I give you. But I decide what I give you. It's all or nothing."

Georgia set her mouth in a tight line, refusing to quit by saying "umbrella". She knew she was still wet as could be—she just hadn't been counting on Jonathan's punishment being quite so...*real*.

Jonathan tickled her clit with one long finger and she moaned as the sensation intensified now that her clit was so swollen and hot from his slaps. He ramped up the rhythm, flicking his finger faster and faster for just a few moments before *slap!* hard on her clit once more. She cried out and she could feel the endorphins rush through as he slapped her pussy again and again, not giving her even a second to recover.

Then he ground his palm into her clit hard—and she came, moaning and gasping for air as the orgasm left her breathless.

"Ready for the whip?" Jonathan asked.

Um, no. Yes. No. Fuck.

Suddenly he was standing over her with a riding crop. Someone must have handed it to him—maybe Casey? "I'm nervous," she whispered.

"I'll give you ten on your ass first to get you used to the sensation before it's applied to your pussy."

He dropped to his knees and quickly uncuffed her ankles and helped her stand. Her knees were weak from the intense orgasm he had just given her.

"Grab the back of the chair, just like Miss Casey did," he ordered.

She did as he said, knowing that every man in the place was now staring at her naked ass. Should that bother her? Because for whatever reason, it really didn't. If anything, it made her even hotter.

"Don't move out of position or I'll start over from one," Jonathan said.

"Okay." She shut her eyes in anticipation.

"One." The riding crop sliced through the air and landed on her right ass cheek and the sheer shock of it made her drop her hands and squat down to the floor.

"Let's try that again, shall we?" Jonathan helped her up. "One."

She gasped as the crop hit her left ass cheek this time,

but she held her position.

"You can always say the safeword, Sweet Georgia," he whispered in her ear.

Hell no!

"Two."

Oh man, she had never before realized just how many ten was. Ten was a lot. By the time he had gotten all the way through to ten licks, her face was sore from grimacing. But amazingly, her pussy was wet. *How did that even happen?*

"You did beautifully," he said and she smiled. She knew she shouldn't care what he thought because he was an arrogant bastard, but knowing she had pleased him made her happy. "Sit back down so I can cuff your ankles apart again."

Oh yeah. They weren't done yet. The thought of the sharp cutting pain of the riding crop being applied to her tender pussy made her tremble with anticipation.

Sitting on her freshly cropped ass hurt. Could she really handle that on her pussy? She lay her head back and stared at the rafters, trying not to think too hard about what was about to happen.

"Georgia," he said, leaning over and peering into her eyes. His voice was soft and for her alone to hear. "Are you okay?"

Was she? Yes. Definitely okay, just weirding herself out. "I'm okay. Thank you."

"I don't think you're ready for this. We'll just save the pussy-whipping for another time."

"No! You can do it, Jonathan. Really."

"I don't think so. We're done—you did great."

She was barely cognizant of the gentlemen in the audience cheering until she felt something light being dropped onto her bare stomach. She opened her eyes and realized that the gentlemen were coming up to her as she lay bound in the chair, her exposed pussy aching from the previous frontal spanking and her ass feeling as though it was on fire from the whipping. Each man dropped a bill onto her breasts or her belly. One man walked up to her and looked at Jonathan, who was standing next to her.

Jonathan nodded to the man as if he were granting him permission or something. The man leaned down and pressed his finger into her pussy, feeling her wetness. Georgia didn't have the energy to protest. Why bother? Just last night it was very likely that same man had spent several minutes licking her pussy, after all.

So why tonight, suddenly, were these men looking to Jonathan for permission to touch her, as if he owned her?

After the impromptu receiving line finished, Jonathan held up the chastity belt and showed it to the men. They clapped and whistled but Georgia started to struggle in the bondage chair.

"Don't even think about putting that on me, Jonathan Syler. I'm serious."

But…oh God. She had to be sick in the head—because she *wanted* him to put it on her.

Jonathan looked at her and smiled as he slid the leather-lined stainless steel chastity belt on to her and the lock clicked into place. "Don't worry, I'll take it off later tonight, when we're alone together."

Georgia shook her head as he uncuffed her aching legs and arms. She stood and stretched as she looked him straight in the eye. "That's a pretty fucked-up way to ask a girl out on a date."

Jonathan laughed. "I'll take you out to dinner and then we can go back to my place."

"You're not giving me much of a choice here," she said. The thought made her pussy throb. "Don't you want a girl to go out with you because she wants to, not because she has to?"

Jonathan stepped up to her so that her bare breasts touched the soft cotton material of his dress shirt. "I don't want just any girl. I want you, however that may be. So yes, if I have to take you against your will, with your pussy and ass locked away from anyone except me, then that's how it will be."

"But you'll unlock me tonight?"

"If you're good."

"What if I'm bad?"

Jonathan laughed. "Even better," he said as he walked off the stage.

* * * * *

Jonathan sat in his black BMW and ran the heat for a few minutes. It wasn't quite cold out yet but the night air definitely had a bit of a chill to it. Georgia finally had finished collecting her cash and was walking down the sidewalk toward his car.

He still couldn't believe he'd found a woman who was as turned-on by wearing a chastity belt as he was by locking her into one. He didn't know what had come over him to make him ask her how she felt about chastity belts. There was something about her, he could tell when he first saw her.

But her response had excited him more than anything else she could possibly have said. Since their fantasies meshed, she was definitely worth getting to know a bit better. If she'd let him.

"Nice car," she said, sliding into the passenger seat.

"Thanks." He put the car in gear. "Are you hungry?"

Georgia shook her head. "Not really." She shifted in her seat as if she were uncomfortable.

"How's that pussy of yours?" he asked, keeping his eyes on the road and the dozens of New Yorkers dodging in and out of traffic.

"Sore, thanks, asshole," she replied lightly.

"Asshole, huh?" He laughed. "You don't know the first thing about sore assholes."

"And I'm pretty sure I never will, thanks."

Huh. Jonathan risked taking his eyes off the road for a moment to look at the beautiful young woman sitting beside him. She was challenging him, but was she doing it on purpose or without even realizing it? Either way, he couldn't let it continue uncontested. "Actually, I am pretty sure you will know quite a bit about sore assholes sooner than you think."

Georgia gasped and laughed. "No I will not!"

"If you want that chastity belt to come off, then yes, you will."

She giggled and Jonathan knew without even looking that she was blushing. *Good.*

He pulled up in front of his building and handed the keys to the valet. "Let's go." He took her arm. "So, where do you want to go to dinner?"

She looked up at him with wide blue eyes. Damn, she was lovely. Lovely, sweet Georgia.

"It's not dinner I'm hungry for," she said coyly.

"You," he said, leaning down to kiss her glossy red lips, "are gorgeous. Let's go upstairs and get that belt off you."

CHAPTER FOUR

Georgia stood in the middle of Jonathan's large kitchen, leaning against the granite countertop. She slipped her heels off and pointed her toes, stretching her calves.

Jonathan stood in front of her and loosened his tie before slowly unbuttoning his dress shirt. She could feel herself getting wet as she watched him strip down to his bare chest.

"Take your clothes off," he said softly as he unbuckled his belt.

The material in her spandex top made a stretching sound—she must have torn a seam in her effort to remove her blouse so quickly. She unzipped her skirt and let it drop around her ankles, kicking it across the cherrywood floor. Why did watching him take off his belt get her so hot?

She waited until he was naked before stepping up to him, letting the small lock at the front of the chastity belt scrape against his thigh as her breasts pressed against his rock-hard abs. He was so tall that his navel wasn't too far below her nipples as she formed her body against his.

She swayed her hips, letting the chastity belt chafe his legs until he groaned and reached down into the pocket of the pants that now lay in a pile on the floor and pulled out the key.

"I'm going to unlock you," he said as he slid the key into the lock and twisted.

He grabbed the metal with both hands and slid it off her, leaving her fully naked before him. She moaned as he pressed his thigh against her clit until she was practically straddling his leg right there in the kitchen.

He lifted her up by the waist as easily as if she weighed nothing at all and she gasped as her ass hit the cold granite countertop. It felt soothing against her still-tender skin. He stepped in between her legs and she smiled as his thick, hard cock came within a millimeter of her pussy.

"Fuck me, Jonathan," she whispered.

"Wait there," he said, stepping back. "Don't move a muscle."

Georgia groaned as he turned and walked over to his pants, which were still in a rumpled pile on the hardwood floor. Did he have any idea how great his ass looked when he bent over like that? She heard the crinkle of cellophane and knew he had put on a condom. Just as quickly as he had stepped away, he was back and pressing his sheathed cock insistently up against her slick pussy.

He grabbed her hips and thrust. She wrapped her legs around his waist and held on to the back of his neck as he withdrew and then buried himself inside her again. He fucked her so hard she was on the verge of coming within moments, letting herself melt into him as he lifted her bodily and walked with her wrapped around him out of the kitchen.

"Where are we going?" she asked, missing his deep thrusts already even though the feeling of him walking with his cock still inside her had a very nice effect as well.

"I don't want to come yet," he said. "And if I keep fucking you like that I will. So I'm taking a break." He stepped through his bedroom door and dropped her onto the bed, where she lay sprawled with her legs open.

"Nooo," she whined. "I don't want to take a break."

He laughed softly. "I said *I* was taking a break. Don't think for a minute that you're going to get a break."

Her eyes widened. *What did that mean?* He flipped her over so her ass was up in the air.

"So," he said, caressing her ass, "were you jealous when I spanked Casey?"

"No," she lied. *How did he know?*

"You have quite a bit to learn about how to deliver a real spanking," he said as his hand came down on her left ass cheek, causing a warm sting. "You were just playing with her, like this," he said, slapping her other ass cheek, warming it but hardly hurting her a bit.

She looked over her shoulder at him and grinned. "I can take it harder than that, Jonathan. You don't need to play nice with me."

He didn't smile, just brought his hand down so hard on her ass that she fell forward from the blow with a shriek. "Really?"

He spanked her again and again until she realized she was crawling forward on the bed to get away from his hard hand. She squealed as he picked her up and threw her over his knee, his hard cock pressing into her lower abdomen as he held her tightly with his arm wrapped around her, one hand buried underneath her and playing with her clit while his other delivered another merciless blow.

"Damn, you have an amazing, amazing ass," he said as he stopped the spanking and just continued to make her writhe over his knee from the constant motion of his fingers on her clit. "Get up," he ordered.

She jumped up, her knees shaky and her ass cheeks burning, and looked at him.

"I want you to get on the bed on your hands and knees—facing away from me."

Okay, that sounded like trouble.

Georgia laughed nervously but did as he said. She felt open and vulnerable kneeling like that in the middle of the bed. Turning to look over her shoulder, she shook her head to get her hair out of her face and watched Jonathan with interest.

He came up behind her and she gasped as his fingers slid deep into her cunt, stroking her carefully.

"Relax around my finger," he said softly, and as soon as he said it Georgia knew what he was up to. Her heartbeat raced as his finger, slick with her wetness, circled her asshole and then pressed forward.

Oh my. That feels incredible. Georgia moaned with pleasure and bucked her hips against his long finger, trying to increase the sensation.

His rhythm faltered and Georgia looked back at him, wanting him to keep going. "Don't stop, I like it," she said.

"Good." He poured a huge dollop of lube over his fingers and dipped two, then three slick digits into her ass.

She moaned, loving every second of it as he carefully prepared her tight channel.

"Come on," she groaned when his fingers slipped out of her asshole. "Fuck me."

"I'm just getting lubed up for you, sweetheart," he said and then the head of his hard cock, slippery as promised and covered in latex, replaced his finger as he eased into her asshole.

A bloom of dark, erotic pain flowed through her as his thick cock stretched her wide. She inhaled sharply, loving the filling sensation as he fucked her slowly and carefully.

"Damn it, Jonathan, I'm not a china doll, *fuck* me!" she said, squealing as he slapped her ass and thrust into her, reaching around and fingering her clit with one hand as he held on to her hip with the other as if he were riding in a rodeo.

Georgia gasped as an orgasm came over her, clenching her muscles around his cock. "Come on me, baby," she gasped. "Rip that condom off and come on me."

He moaned at her words, pumping only a few more times until he pulled out of her with a grunt and ejaculated on the small of her back.

His cum sat on her spine like a puddle of warm syrup and she stayed in position on her hands and knees, breathing deeply and focusing on that one warm spot as the aftershocks of her orgasm washed through her.

"Sorry about that," Jonathan murmured as he used what was probably four hundred thread count Egyptian cotton sheets to wipe his sticky cum from her back.

She laughed and rolled onto her side, pulling him down next to her. "Don't be sorry, I like it. I begged for it, remember?"

"You like my cum on your body?"

"Love it."

Jonathan smiled and kissed her. "Tonight was fun."

Georgia nodded and looked into his gorgeous brown eyes. "I promise you I'll see you again—you don't need to put the chastity belt on me."

It was true—he didn't need to. But she wanted him to. Could he see it on her face, in her expression?

Jonathan shook his head. "I believe you want to see me again. What I don't believe is that you have the self-control not to masturbate while you're not with me."

She sat up. How did he know her so well already, when they were practically strangers? "Oh all right," she sighed.

He raised his eyebrows. "You mean you'll consent to wearing the chastity belt again?"

"Yes. For you, yes. Since it's obviously so important to you," she said. *And I want to make you happy.*

His smile then was worth the inconvenience. "That's wonderful. Thank you," he said, grabbing her hand in his and kissing it reverently.

"Can I go clean up first?"

"Of course," he said, gesturing toward the bathroom. "And since you like anal play so much, I'm going to reward you for consenting to the chastity belt by putting a butt plug in you before I lock you up. I have a very large one that I think you're ready for."

Georgia's mouth dropped open. "You want me to wear a plug all night?"

"I told you earlier that you were going to learn a thing or two about sore assholes, didn't I?"

She laughed. Damn, this man was something else, that was for sure.

"That thing is huge," she said, eyeing the plug warily.

It had to be several inches thick at its widest part. Much, much thicker than his cock, and that was saying a lot.

"Let's let gravity do the work then," he said, walking to the corner and pulling a straight-backed wood chair away from the wall. With a flourish, he removed the small pillow from the back of the chair and stuck the base of the butt plug to the seat.

"You can't be serious," she said as he poured lube in his hand and stroked it over the plug, which sat erect on the chair somehow. He wobbled its firm, rubbery length but it didn't tip over. Must be suctioned.

"Just hover over it," he said, "and lower yourself nice and slow."

Georgia stood over the chair as if she were ready to sit and spread her thighs, lowering herself until she felt the tip of the plug slide into her asshole. Not so bad. She dropped lower and gasped as her sphincter spread wide, her thigh muscles burning as she forced herself to go as slowly as humanly possible.

"It's too wide," she said, frozen in place three-quarters of the way down the plug. Her quads trembled with exertion.

"Allow me," Jonathan said. He put his hand on her shoulder and, while he definitely wasn't pushing her down, simply having his hand guide her gave her the courage to continue. He dropped his hand to her nipple and caressed it, flicking it lightly.

She gasped as her ass cheeks hit the wood chair and grinned. "It's in." Georgia sat up carefully, easily breaking the suction seal the base of the plug had made with the chair. "Oh wow." She felt *full*—and it felt amazing.

Jonathan smiled and patted her bottom, spreading her cheeks, fingering the flared base sticking out. "Gorgeous," he murmured. "I'll put the belt on you and I want you to spend the night."

"Really? Are we ready for that?"

"It's just one night, Georgia. I'm not asking you to move in or anything."

She blushed. Of course. No biggie. "If you lock me up in the belt, how will we consummate our first all-nighter together?" she teased.

"I'll just have to be a gentleman," he said, picking the chastity belt up off the floor.

Her stomach fluttered pleasantly as he clicked the metal into place. There was something about this chastity belt that was growing on her—the feeling of being *his*.

The fact that she had the plug in her and couldn't remove it until Jonathan gave her permission and physically unlocked her was such a turn-on that she stepped up to him, suddenly needing to feel him between her legs once more—but she couldn't slake her desire with another orgasm. Not with the belt on.

She looked up at him. "We can still kiss, though, can't we?"

His lips against hers, hot and sweet, were answer enough. "You, Sweet Georgia, really are a glutton for punishment."

Jonathan actually ended up removing the chastity belt in the middle of the night, pulling the plug out with excruciating slowness as she moaned in the dark. But before she could come again, he locked her back up. She wailed in frustration but he kissed her cheek and told her he'd take care of her at the club the following evening.

Georgia woke up to Jonathan's alarm clock buzzing. She rolled over sleepily, but Jonathan jumped out of bed and opened the drapes, letting the sunshine stream in over her face.

"You're welcome to stay if you want," he said, "but I've got to go to work."

"No, I'll go," she said, rubbing the sleep from her eyes. She winced as she looked at the white cotton pillowcase, which was now smeared with her black eye makeup. "I'm sorry."

Jonathan laughed. "The housekeeper's coming today anyway, she'll do the laundry. It's nothing she hasn't seen before."

Oh. Of course. She tried to smile to cover the inexplicable disappointment she felt. What did she expect? He obviously wasn't a virgin. And neither was she.

"Come here so I can unlock you," he said.

She rolled out of the bed and walked over to him, naked except for the chastity belt. "You don't have to unlock me."

He laughed. "I need to check your skin and make sure everything's okay," he said as he unlocked the belt and pulled it off her. "After you shower I'll put it back on you. I told you it was staying on for a week, and I don't make promises I can't keep."

"Yeah, that's probably a good idea," she said, sighing with pleasure when his fingers gently caressed her labia as he inspected her inch by inch. "There's no way I'll have the self-control not to masturbate before tonight otherwise."

"Go shower," he said, giving her a quick smack on the butt. "I'll make coffee."

* * * * *

Jonathan watched as she sashayed into the bathroom. How had this turned so quickly into...whatever the hell it was? First she was pissed that he put the chastity belt on her—that he could understand, because even though she had told him the idea turned her on, he knew the reality was a bit more daunting than the fantasy.

What was a little more difficult to get, though, was

what exactly had happened that made her sing in the shower, ready to come out and allow him to lock her up again?

She *wanted* the chastity belt, there was no denying that, despite her halfhearted protests. He certainly hadn't counted on finding a woman like Georgia. It was a bit disconcerting—but he had to admit that knowing she was willingly submitting to his fetish turned him on. There was something about this woman—he had known it the moment he saw her, despite the fact that she had been spread-eagle and being licked by every gentleman in GC. Or hell, maybe because of it. Sex would never be boring with Georgia.

The shower was running when he knocked on the bathroom door.

"Come in, water's fine!" Georgia called.

Jonathan grinned and stripped off his T-shirt. He had time to get her primed for this evening before he had to leave for work. The shower door was steamed up but Georgia turned and pressed her tits against the glass, giving him an instant erection.

She was so beautiful with the lather from the shampoo streaming down her breasts, over her tight, flat stomach. Stepping into the hot spray, Jonathan took the soap from her hands and gently washed her, turning her in his arms to let the water rinse the bubbles off.

"Spread your thighs," he whispered, dropping to his knees on the cold, wet tiles. Water dribbled in his mouth from the shower as he licked her freshly shaved pussy, darting his tongue between her lips to capture her clitoris.

She moaned, her hands tangling in his wet hair as he sucked hard, rolling the little nub between his teeth and tongue.

Then he stood.

"No, keep going, I was so close," she groaned.

"I know," he said wickedly. "Now I'm going to put the belt back on you."

Georgia's mouth dropped open and Jonathan shut off the shower and grabbed a towel. "You have to finish what you started," she said. "You can't leave me like this all day!"

"Sweet Georgia," he said, running the towel over her body, "that's exactly what I intend to do. It will make tonight at the club that much more enjoyable for us all."

To his surprise, she started fingering herself, rubbing her clit as fast as her hand would allow. She was trying to cheat herself to an orgasm before he could get the chastity belt back on her.

Laughing, he grabbed her wrists in one hand. "Oh no you don't, you little minx."

Georgia cried out in frustration, pounding her fists against his muscular chest in protest as he carried her still-wet body into the bedroom. "No, you jerk! Let me come first," she insisted as he clicked the chastity belt into place once more.

"I'll see you tonight," he said. He dressed quickly, arranging his tie with the precision of a man who learned long ago the art of the perfect knot.

"What's going to happen tonight?"

"It'll be an experience you'll never forget, sweetheart, I promise you that."

Georgia sighed and looked down at the belt. "You're such an asshole."

She clearly needed release so badly, but her clit was locked away now from even herself.

Perfect.

* * * * *

Georgia's phone chimed once later that afternoon when she was trying to nap. She had to be bright-eyed for this evening's adventure at the GC, whatever it may be. Maybe another hour of forced orgasms? She knew if that was the case she'd be begging to get out of it after fifteen minutes or so, but right now the thought sounded so good she could almost climax just thinking about the last time.

Picking up her cell, she scanned the text message lazily before bolting upright on the couch. *You better get over here. The cops are here asking about you.* It was from Vincent!

She texted back, *What do they want? Which officer?*

A chime and then the last name she ever wanted to see again came across her cell phone screen. *Officer Ramirez. Just get here.*

What did her ex-boyfriend want with her now? She hadn't broken any laws. And he sure as hell knew they weren't getting back together. So why was he asking Vincent about her?

Fuck.

* * * * *

Mary Ann greeted her at the door. "Thank God you're here," she said, her eyebrows creased with worry. "That damn cop won't leave until he sees you're okay."

Vincent came up behind Mary Ann and gestured Georgia inside. His face was stony and expressionless, but anger seethed out of his pores.

"I didn't call the cops, Vincent," Georgia said. "You know I wouldn't do something like that."

He sighed. "Just go talk to him."

Georgia walked into the back office. Mary Ann and Vincent waited in the lounge behind her. Her ex-boyfriend Eric Ramirez stood in his police blues, arms at his sides.

He shook his head. "I was told the lady in question was called 'Sweet Georgia'. I can't believe it's actually *you*. Jesus."

"Hi, Eric."

"I'm on the job. Call me Officer," he said. "And close the door. We need to talk."

Closing the office door, she laughed to cover her nerves and sat on the couch. "Gimme a break, *Officer*. What the hell are you doing here?"

"We got a concerned call from a client here. Said a man locked you into a chastity belt against your will and wouldn't take it off."

Georgia shook her head. "Not true."

Eric stepped toward her and Georgia gasped as he lifted her skirt. "Get away from me, Eric, I mean it."

"Jesus, Georgia," he said in apparent disgust when he saw the metal contraption hiding under her clothes. "Why the fuck did this pervert do this to you? Were you such a slut he had to forcibly lock you up?"

"Get out of here," she said, struggling to hide her flushed face as she lowered her skirt.

"While I can see where the guy who put the chastity belt on you was going with this, I'm still going to arrest his ass." Eric looked down at his paper and read the name. "Jonathan Syler. He's going down."

"There was no crime, you idiot!" she yelled, jumping to her feet in outrage. "I slept at his house last night and I practically *begged* him to put the belt back on me. I like being his."

Eric tilted his head and leaned back against Vincent's expensive mahogany desk. "I received a phone call saying that this guy put the belt on you and wouldn't unlock it, against your will. Are you saying that never happened?"

"Well, m-maybe at first," she stuttered, "but now it's different."

"So Jonathan Syler did indeed restrain you against your will."

"Damn it, Eric, you're twisting my words. Anyway, I'm not pressing charges, so get the fuck out of here."

"Are you in a relationship with this man?"

Was she? "Yes."

"I think I'm going to arrest him anyway," Eric said. "It's like with domestic abuse, sometimes the wife won't talk but if there's evidence we can still convict."

Georgia wanted to scream in frustration. She sat on the couch and put her face in her hands. "There's no evidence, Officer Moron. You're just doing this to fuck with my head."

"Oh, there's no evidence?" He stood above her, glaring

down from his full height. "How about a room full of men watching you get assaulted? How about the fact that you are *wearing* a damned chastity belt right fucking *now*?"

"Please, please, Eric...Officer. Seriously—I'm fine. Just don't screw this up for me."

"Don't screw what up?" he asked exasperatedly.

"I just—I think I might be falling in love with him," she whispered.

Eric shook his head. "You are one messed-up girl. I'm lucky you left me when you did." He walked past her and opened the door. "Seriously, Georgia—come by the station if you need help. We could get that thing off you if you need us to."

Georgia looked up in surprise. *Since when was Eric nice?* "Th-thanks. But I'm fine."

He left, closing the door behind him, leaving Georgia sitting there, trembling. Why had she said that—was it even true?

Could she really be falling for Jonathan so quickly?

CHAPTER FIVE

"Gentlemen," Vincent purred into the microphone from the GC stage, "for your viewing pleasure—I present Casey and Sweet Georgia!"

Georgia laughed at the intro and came onstage holding Casey's hand, swinging it slightly as the stage fright kicked in—just a bit of butterflies she had unsuccessfully tried to drown in scotch moments earlier. Thank God the spotlight on them was bright enough Georgia couldn't see into the audience. She could hear the men though, the ice clinking in their glasses.

Was Jonathan out there? Watching her?

The thought made her wet.

Tossing her hair, she laughed as Casey lifted their hands up high between them in a victory pose as they hit their mark—a little *x* of duct tape on the stage where the light was perfect. What was going to happen? She had been offered two hundred plus tips to perform with Casey, doing some girl-on-girl action for the men. But the details were a little hazy.

Vincent nodded to Casey, who leaned in and whispered in Georgia's ear. "I'm going to undress you, okay?"

Georgia nodded, feeling slightly buzzed from the

scotch. Definitely not drunk. Mary Ann had warned her not to get so hammered that she'd regret anything she did at the club. Good advice from a woman who was starting to have almost a maternal influence in her life.

Casey let go of Georgia's hand long enough to slowly unbutton Georgia's sheer, flimsy blouse, letting it fall to the stage floor. A few men cat-called and she her face flushed with heat. *Let 'em watch.* It turned her on.

Georgia stepped toward Casey and kissed her deep on the mouth, loving the taste of her friend's strawberry lip-gloss. Kissing a girl was so…different from kissing a man. No stubble, for one. Softer lips, for another. And while in Jonathan's arms she felt entirely submissive and feminine, in Casey's she enjoyed feeling the other girl's femininity surround her. Her hair smelled amazing, like citrus shampoo.

Pulling her bra straps off her shoulders one by one, Georgia waited until the hollering in the audience had calmed before unhooking the bra completely, causing the men to start up all over again as her breasts were bared. Smiling, Casey dipped her head and pulled one of Georgia's rouged nipples into her mouth, sucking daintily.

Rouged nipples. That was another trick Mary Ann had taught her—a little red lipstick on the mouth, a smudge on her areolas. The men loved it. Georgia gasped as Casey flicked her tongue around and around her sensitive tip.

Casey reached behind her and unzipped the back of Georgia's miniskirt, letting it fall around her ankles, leaving her body bare except for the chastity belt. Casey sank to her knees dramatically and looked out into the audience.

As if on cue, Vincent handed her the mic.

"Oh no," Casey cried into the microphone, playing it up for the men. "My Sweet Georgia, you're all locked up!"

Georgia laughed and shrugged, like, *what can I do?*

"Mr. Syler," Casey said, "won't you please come unlock my friend so we can play?"

The audience clapped as Jonathan stood. Georgia

couldn't see him past the spotlight, but she imagined him setting his drink down and wiping the condensation from the glass on a napkin before taking off his Armani suit jacket.

Those butterflies fluttered in her stomach again as she watched him climb the few steps up to the stage. He was so damn good-looking.

He took the little metal key out of his pocket and she grinned. She needed to come so badly, especially after what he had done to her this morning, leaving her need unrequited like that and her with no way to fulfill her desire.

Her pussy felt so bare and exposed when the belt came off and suddenly she was acutely aware that she was stark naked on a stage.

Jonathan whispered in Casey's ear and she giggled and nodded. Then he was gone, standing off in the wings, watching.

"Stand still, Sweet Georgia," Casey said, "so I can play with your little pussy just like Mr. Syler told me to."

Finally. She was so ready to come she thought she might die from it.

Closing her eyes, Georgia let her head drop back with pleasure as Casey knelt in front of her, carefully parting her labia with her fingers. She was so amped up that any weirdness she might have felt about getting physical with her girlfriend was the farthest thing from her mind.

Casey was petting her slowly, barely making contact with her nether lips and avoiding her clit completely.

Groaning, Georgia said, "More."

"Naughty, naughty," Casey said in a singsong voice. "Don't you get it yet, Georgia?"

Georgia's head snapped up and her eyes flew open as Jonathan came up behind her and held her against his muscular body, her naked flesh pressed against the fine silk of his tie and the soft cotton of his button-down shirt.

"I'm going to hold you here," he murmured in her ear,

his breath hot on her cheek, "while Casey teases you."

"But," Casey said, running her fingers over Georgia's inner thighs, "I'm under strict orders not to let you climax."

"No!" Georgia cried, struggling to free herself from Jonathan's strong grasp. "You can't do this to me, you gotta let me come, I need it."

Jonathan held her tight and chuckled. "This will be good for you," he said. "And good to watch."

Vincent roared into the microphone, "Tease and denial, gentlemen, tease and denial! How much can Sweet Georgia take?"

Until he spoke, Georgia had almost forgotten she was getting paid for her performance. *Oh hell, how bad could it be?* She could take anything, right?

Or not. She gasped as Casey's tongue flicked out and tapped her clit for one delicious moment before retreating into her mouth. After a moment the sensation subsided and out came her tongue again. *Tap. Tap.* Then nothing.

"Lift your leg," Jonathan ordered, and Georgia laid her head back on his chest as she slowly raised one leg, just like she had learned in ballet class as a girl.

Jonathan grabbed hold of her calf, securing it in the crook of his arm, and she felt off balance, like a dancer in a strange pose—one leg on the floor, the other pointing to the stage lights in the rafters.

And now her pussy was completely open to Casey's merciless ministrations.

"I have a surprise for you," Casey said, and though Georgia couldn't see her friend's face when she turned to the audience, Georgia was sure Casey had just winked at the men. She was holding something up—what was it?

A feather? Oh no...*a feather!*

"Nooooo," Georgia moaned when Casey touched the pointed quill tip to her clit, tickling her steadily without building up any rhythm. She squirmed desperately, writhing against Jonathan's chest as the teasing continued.

There was no pressure, no satisfaction to be gleaned from the maddening sensations overwhelming her nerve endings.

"Stop," she cried, "I'll die." She bucked her hips as best she could in her awkward position, alternating between trying to gain further contact with the feather and trying to escape it.

Casey threw her head back and laughed. "No one ever died from not getting an orgasm, silly girl." The men laughed appreciatively with her.

Damn her! Damn Jonathan. This was his doing. He was torturing her on purpose. She was going to say "umbrella" and call this whole thing off—but she was so close to coming, she could feel it. If only Casey would keep that up for one more second—

"Damn you!" she yelled as Casey abruptly switched motions with a giggle.

Oh she was right on the edge…just a little pressure right on her clit and she would explode…but all she felt was the lightest touch, not nearly enough to push her over the edge. Her pulse was racing and her nerve endings felt so frayed she wondered briefly if anyone actually *had* died from not being allowed to come. Because it certainly felt that way right now.

She was going to come, she was going to come— Georgia gasped as she felt the beginning of a contraction and then all sensation stopped. The chastity belt locked in place around her hips and Georgia wailed in frustration as she dropped to her knees on the stage floor, nearly in tears.

"You can't do this to me," she said. "Please, please."

Jonathan looked down at her and smiled thoughtfully. "Are you mine, Sweet Georgia?"

She looked up at him and nodded. "I'm yours, all yours."

It wasn't even part of her performance. Fuck it. She was done performing. This was about her and Jonathan.

Even Casey didn't matter right now. Those men in the audience certainly didn't either.

"If you're mine, then you'll want to please me. Do you want to please me?"

Georgia nodded and reached for his zipper, sure that was what he wanted.

"No," he said, restraining her hand.

"Make me come," she pleaded.

Jonathan merely shook his head and walked off the stage. She had disappointed him somehow.

"Fuck you," she called after him. "Umbrella." She stood up clumsily, looking around the stage for Vincent. "Umbrella, Vincent. I'm fucking done here. Now get this motherfucking belt off of me."

The men booed good-naturedly as Georgia stumbled naked off the stage, with Casey on her heels.

Vincent didn't seem too upset that she said the safeword, he just shook her hand and gave her a hundred-dollar bill.

"What's this for?" Georgia asked warily. "I said the safeword. I broke the contract."

"I like your act, Sweet Georgia. You're always welcome back here."

Oh. "Thanks, Vincent."

"I don't have a key for that thing though," he said. "You gotta take that up with Jonathan."

Hell no. She was going to have to go to the only person she knew who would actually take the belt off her without hesitation. Her ex, the cop.

* * * * *

Georgia pushed open the door to the police station and nodded to the lady at the front desk, who waved in surprised recognition. She must have remembered her from the times she had stopped by the station when she and Erik were dating.

"Is Erik here?" she asked without preamble.

"Officer Ramirez?" the woman replied. "I'll let him

know you're here. Have a seat, dear."

Georgia ignored her, preferring to stand. She had too much anger built up just to sit there and twiddle her thumbs.

A door on the side opened and Erik looked at her, raising his eyebrows. "Come around back," he said, holding the door for her.

"Thanks."

Erik brushed a speck of imaginary lint off his pristine uniform and pulled a chair out for her but Georgia just shook her head.

"Lemme guess. I need to go get some bolt cutters."

"Yup. I need this thing off me, now."

Erik's jaw tightened. "I'll be right back."

Sighing, Georgia leaned up against the edge of the desk and waited. "Finally," she breathed in relief when he came back moments later holding a pair of heavy-duty red-handled bolt cutters.

"I'm gonna kill this Syler asshole," Erik said as she lifted her skirt up.

Holding the belt away from her skin as far as he could, he clipped the side, grunting with exertion as it took him a few tries to cut through the thick metal. Georgia was able to release the chastity belt and let it drop to the floor.

She quickly covered her bare flesh with her skirt.

And then a lump formed in her throat. *What have I done?*

She'd acted way too hastily... After practically begging Jonathan to put the belt on her, she'd betrayed him in a moment of weakness.

This chastity belt wasn't for Jonathan—it was for her. Because she fantasized about it, about being under Jonathan's lock and key.

And now... She'd messed up big time.

Freedom didn't feel nearly as good as she'd imagined it would. Who was she kidding, anyway? She didn't want to be free. She wanted to be Jonathan's.

Erik looked ready to chew nails. "I've got his address."

"What are you talking about it? I'm not pressing charges, I told you."

Erik frowned, the muscle in his jaw twitching. "That rich asshole is gonna pay for doing this to you. You may not be my girl anymore, but I'm gonna punch his teeth in for trying to make you his bitch."

Shit. "No, Erik, it's fine, just let it go."

But Erik was already out the door. Georgia ran after him. "Stop, Erik!"

In the parking lot, Erik walked fast, ignoring her as he jumped into his police car. "Stop following me, Georgia. This isn't something for a girl to see."

Fuck that! It was rush hour—she could actually get to Jonathan's apartment quicker taking the subway. Georgia ran to the nearest subway station and raced through the turnstile, grateful for her full MetroCard. She ran down the track toward the train, groaning inwardly as she had to wait for the throng of people to exit before she could enter the subway car.

Picking up her cell phone, she called Jonathan to warn him. No answer. Of course. Why would he want to talk to her now?

Keeping one hand on the bar above her head and the other on her phone, she texted, *My ex is gonna beat you up.* Damn it. That sounded like a threat, not the warning she intended it to be.

Be careful, she texted again. Not much better, but better than nothing.

* * * * *

Jonathan shook his head in amusement when he got Georgia's texts. That girl was unglued. And to think he had thought she might be the one for him.

Hell, who was he kidding? She *was* the one for him. There was no denying it. No one else turned him on so completely and fulfilled his fetish with such passion as she did. No one else had her devil-may-care attitude and sweet, beautiful eyes that seemed to show directly into her soul.

Thoughts of Georgia consumed him.

There was a knock at the door. More of a pounding, really. Angry pounding. Jonathan peered through the peephole and saw a cop standing there, looking pissed.

"Can I help you, Officer?" he asked.

"It's Ramirez," the cop said. "I'm not on official business. I'm here about Georgia."

"Then you'll understand why I don't want to let you in," Jonathan said.

"Listen to me, you piece of shit," the cop barked. "You ever lock up my girlfriend again and I will hunt you down—"

"Jonathan," Georgia's voice came through the door. "Don't open—"

What was she doing here? He opened the door, not wanting to leave her out there with that psycho cop, but as soon as he turned the handle, Ramirez pushed his way inside, dragging Georgia by the hand.

"Let her go," Jonathan said.

The cop let her hand go, but now he looked ready to pounce on Jonathan.

"Come on, guys," Georgia said. "It's over. Done."

"Did you sic your ex on me just because I wouldn't let you come?" Jonathan asked incredulously.

She dropped her head into her hands and sighed. "Maybe. I'm sorry. I didn't think he'd actually hunt you down."

Ramirez looked from her to Jonathan and shook his head in disgust. "Georgia, you deserve better than this guy."

"This is the guy I want," she said, gesturing to Jonathan. "I know it sounds crazy, Erik, but I never should have come to you to cut off the chastity belt."

Jonathan felt under her skirt. No belt. "You had another man take off the belt I put on you?" he asked softly.

Never mind the fact that he had paid a fortune for that

chastity belt and had fantasized for ages about the moment he would find the right woman to wear it. She had betrayed him by destroying the belt.

"I'm sorry," she said. "I don't know what I was thinking. I was upset. I was crazy frustrated and not thinking clearly, you know? But I don't need that chastity belt anymore—because I'll do whatever you say, Jonathan. I mean it. I'm yours...at least, I *want* to be yours."

The cop snorted. "Good luck with that." He turned and started to walk out, but he stopped at the door and glared at Jonathan. "Listen, Syler. I know where you live. I know where you play. And if I ever hear that you hurt her or even breathed on her funny, I will take you down. *Comprende, amigo?*"

Jonathan nodded as Ramirez left, slamming the door. He could respect that. Hell, if Georgia ever left him and he found out that her new man had upset her, he'd want to kill them too.

And he didn't want Georgia ever to leave him. She was unlike any woman he had ever known. But how could they fix things now that she had gone behind his back like that? To her ex-boyfriend.

Georgia sank to her knees in front of him and looked up at him, tears running down her face, her blonde hair disheveled. "I'm sorry," she said again. "Can you forgive me?"

She was so beautiful like that, it took every ounce of willpower he had not to pick her up off the carpet and kiss away her tears.

"I suppose I pushed you too hard," he conceded. "You weren't ready for that last performance."

"I'm ready now," she said. "Do whatever you want to me. I'm yours. If you tell me never to masturbate again without your permission I'll do it for you, in a heartbeat."

Touching her cheek, he carefully wiped away the mascara smudged under her eyes. "That is an incredible gift," he said. "But how do I know that you won't just throw a tantrum and run back to your ex again?"

Even as he said it he could see the answer in her eyes. She wanted to make him happy—and seeing that made him desire her even more.

"I-I'm—" she stammered, losing her words as he finally gave in to temptation and lifted her off the floor.

"Forget it," he whispered. "I don't need apologies. Let's just move forward. I want to be with you, to see how this all pans out."

Her smile lit up her face and Jonathan laughed, hugging her tightly.

"Jonathan?" she said. "I...um, never actually came, you know. When I went to see Erik he took the belt off but he didn't touch me. And I didn't touch myself."

"Really..." he murmured, sliding his hand down her ass and then up under her skirt. Her pussy was bare and slick with need.

"What would you say if I told you I was going to play with you for hours as punishment for what you did?" he asked, running his fingers over her swollen nub. "What would you do if I told you I would keep you on the edge and not let you come?"

Her breath caught and she made a choked sound as if she was holding back a cry of frustration but she nodded. "I understand. I'll take whatever you give me—I'm yours, Jonathan."

"Good girl, Sweet Georgia," he whispered, rubbing her clit faster now. "But I'll give you what you need."

Thank God.

She moaned as he lifted her up and tossed her onto the leather couch, shoving her skirt up her thighs as he knelt before her. Locking her ankles behind his neck, Georgia cried out as he ate her pussy hungrily, sucking her clit into his mouth and tonguing it with relish.

Her body trembled as the orgasm rocked her, sending wave after wave of contractions through her womb. She gasped as the aftershocks hit her and Jonathan kept his position, laving her pussy even as she halfheartedly pushed his head away.

"I need my cock in you," he said. "Now."

Dizzy with desire, she fumbled with his fly and kissed his cock passionately when it sprang out of his pants, fully erect and throbbing in her hand.

He groaned as she started to take his length into her mouth but shook his head, gently pulling her up off the couch. "Get on your hands and knees," he said.

Georgia did as he said, loving his commanding tone. She gasped as his hand slapped her ass cheek. "Ow!"

"Don't you think you deserve a spanking?" he asked, spanking first one cheek and then the other with enough sting to make her jump.

"Yeah," she agreed. "I do deserve a spanking, but... *Ouch!*"

He spanked her again, harder this time, until she couldn't think of anything else except her burning bottom and his dominance over her body. "Your ass is all pink now," he said, rubbing the hurt away with gentle full palm strokes. "It's gorgeous."

His hands gripped her hips and she wiggled against him, feeling her warm, freshly spanked flesh against his muscular abdomen. She was so wet, so turned-on and oh so ready for him.

He drove into her cunt, fucking her deeply as she moaned in pleasure with each hard thrust. Her G-spot was being hit so perfectly that within moments she was melting around his cock, climaxing even as he continued to fuck her.

In the throes of orgasm, she cried out his name over and over. She'd never get sick of being loved like this. Whatever her future held, she wanted Jonathan to be part of it.

He rolled her over onto her back and carefully extricated himself. "Keep your legs spread just like that," he said. He got up and came back over, holding the riding crop in his hand. "I think you're ready for this now."

Georgia nodded, staring into his intense brown eyes as he brought the crop down directly on her tender pussy. She squealed and slammed her thighs tightly together.

"Let's try it again," he said. "But this time I want you not to make a sound. Don't close your thighs after—keep them spread for me. I want you to thank me after I whip your pussy—and I want you to mean it."

She nodded and took a deep breath as the crop sliced through the air and hit her clit. The pain cut through her, flooding her with a wave of endorphins that left her breathless.

No crying. No sound. Keeping her legs open, she looked at Jonathan, at his handsome face. "Thank you."

He smiled and tossed the riding crop onto the floor.

EPILOGUE

One Year Later

Vincent and Mary Ann greeted Georgia with delight when she stopped by one evening after school.

"We've missed you, Sweet Georgia," Vincent said, kissing her cheek. "Some of the gentlemen still ask after you."

"Aww, that's nice," she said, laughing. "It was fun while it lasted, but ever since Jonathan stopped coming here we figured it would probably be best for me to just focus on studying."

"That's right! Casey said you were in nursing school," Mary Ann said. "How's that going?"

"Speak of the devil," Vincent said as Casey bounded over to them and hugged Georgia exuberantly.

"It's hard, but it's worth it," Georgia said in response to Mary Ann. "I love my rotations, so far at least. Ready, Case?"

"I was born ready," Casey said, grabbing her hand and blowing a kiss to Vincent over her shoulder. "I'll be back in time for tonight's show," she called.

"When are you gonna quit this place?" Georgia muttered under her breath as they climbed into her car in the parking lot.

"We can't all be nurses, hon," Casey said, grinning. "Besides, I love it. Performing, I mean. And the money is insane, you know that."

Georgia shrugged. The Gentlemen's Club had definitely served its purpose for her, but now she was done. Ready to take the next step and move forward in her life. She had even moved in with Jonathan six months ago, which was a big deal for both of them.

Her phone chimed and she handed it to Casey since she couldn't text and drive at the same time. Hell, she could barely listen to the radio and drive at the same time. Driving required a lot more concentration than riding a subway, that was for sure.

"What's it say?"

Casey grabbed her phone and giggled. "It says 'Casey is welcome to join us tonight if you're up for it'."

"Jonathan texted that?"

"No, Vincent did," she said sarcastically. Laughing, Casey's thumbs flew over the tiny keyboard.

"Hey—what'd you write?" Georgia resisted the urge to take her eyes off the road.

"I wrote, 'Casey is so hot, we might just start without you'."

Georgia laughed. "I think you just earned me a spanking."

"Oooh, maybe Jonathan will let me be the one who administers it."

"I hope so, because he spanks hard." Georgia pulled up to their building and handed the keys to the valet, grinning at her friend. "We really have to do this more often."

Inside, Casey held the elevator for her and pressed the PH button. "You know you can call me whenever—you guys are the cutest couple to play with."

A cute couple, huh? It was becoming less and less strange to think of herself as part of a couple now, actually. Jonathan was her soul mate—that much she knew. And the sex never got old. She loved that he was totally willing to be monogamous with her and still let her invite her friend over to play, even if she didn't want *him* to touch anyone but her. What could she say? She got jealous.

But Casey was the perfect playmate for their infrequent ménages, because Casey had no problem respecting boundaries, even the strange ones.

Jonathan greeted them at the door and kissed both girls, Casey on the cheek and Georgia on the lips. "Glad you could come," he said.

"Well, I haven't come yet," Casey joked.

"Let's remedy that immediately," Jonathan said, pouring himself a scotch on the rocks. "Drink?"

Georgia shook her head but then took Jon's glass from his hand and sipped it, making a face as the alcohol burned her throat.

"Casey?" Jonathan handed her his glass to sip from as well but Casey shook her head. "Okay then, why don't you take off those lovely tight pants and lie back on the couch."

Casey grinned and wriggled out of her pants. "How 'bout the thong?"

This time Georgia answered. "Off."

The thong fell on the carpet next to her pants and Casey sat on the leather couch.

Jonathan led Georgia by the hand over to the couch and gently guided her to her knees between Casey's naked legs.

"Eat her," he said, his voice low.

Georgia looked at the freshly waxed bare pussy in front of her face, reaching her fingers out to separate the thick outer lips to reveal the fleshy folds within. Pressing her lips to Casey's clitoris, she kissed her softly first before letting her tongue explore her cunt.

Casey moaned, which enticed Georgia to suck her clit into her mouth harder, flicking the swollen nub with her tongue over and over.

"Raise your hips," Jonathan told Georgia as he lay on the carpet and positioned himself beneath her slick pussy, "and sit on my face."

Georgia did as he said, sighing with pleasure as she balanced above his face. He held her hips tightly as he licked her clit and Georgia threw her head back with a gasp.

Suddenly his hand left her hip and slapped her ass cheek. "Don't even think about leaving Casey hanging. Keep going—eat her pussy."

Georgia went back between Casey's thighs, sliding her tongue around every crevice. She could barely concentrate because her mind kept going to her own pleasure as Jonathan kept his mouth latched on to her clit. But the moment she paused to let a wave of sensation wash through her, his hard palm brought her back to the task at hand.

Not that she minded—not in the least. Casey was delicious, and the fact that Jonathan got off on seeing her eat out her girlfriend made it all the more enjoyable.

Casey bucked her hips wildly as she came, and Georgia had to hold her hips still so she could continue eating her out as the orgasm rocked her body.

"Don't stop, I don't care if she came once—keep licking her," Jonathan warned before delving back into Georgia's pussy.

She cried out as the pleasure overtook her and she came hard, grinding her hips over his face, trying to keep her mouth attached to Casey's pussy at the same time.

Jonathan gave her one final nibble before sliding out from underneath Georgia's hips. "Get up, sweetheart," he said as he stood behind her, his cock tantalizingly close to her pussy. "I want Casey to kiss you so she can see how good she tastes."

Casey smiled and grabbed Georgia's face, bringing her in close for a passionate kiss. "Is that what I taste like?" she asked, laughing.

"I love it," Georgia admitted. "But I really need cock to get me going…ahem, ahem," she said, looking over her shoulder to Jonathan like, *get a move on, let's go.*

"Subtle," Jonathan said as he drove into her from behind. Georgia inhaled sharply and dropped her lips to Casey's nipples, covering them with ferocious kisses as Jonathan stroked her G-spot over and over.

Casey gasped and slid her hand between her legs to play with her own clit while Georgia teased her breasts. "It's so much fun watching you guys fuck," she said. "Can we still do this sometimes even after you get married?"

Georgia looked up from Casey's ample chest and raised an eyebrow, shaking her head as if to clear her thoughts while Jonathan continued fucking her. "Who says we're getting married?"

She looked over her shoulder at Jonathan just as he was making the "cut it out" sign, drawing his finger across his neck.

Casey giggled. "Oops. I thought he said something already. Never mind."

Jonathan grunted and pulled out, ejaculating on Georgia's bottom. "Nice, Casey. You did that on purpose."

"Sorry." She didn't look sorry though. She looked positively pleased with herself.

"Georgia, don't move. Casey's going to clean you off—with her tongue. Maybe that will keep her from talking too much."

Casey jumped off the couch and came around behind Georgia. "Oh girl, your ass is just splattered with cum," she said, laughing. "I may be back here awhile."

Jonathan took Casey's place on the couch and watched them. Georgia liked the feel of Casey's warm little tongue darting all over her ass cheek, even if it did tickle.

"She thought you already said something about what?" Georgia asked, wiggling a little as Casey's tongue became very tickly for a moment.

"All right, I guess now is as a good a time as any. Because the answer, Casey, is yes—we can still do this after we get married."

Georgia turned and looked at Casey with a confused expression as Casey sat back on her haunches and cheered.

"Um, aren't you forgetting something?" Georgia said drily as she got up and sat naked on Jonathan's lap.

"Yeah, like asking her," Casey pointed out.

Jonathan laughed. "Hang on, I have to get the ring." He picked Georgia up piggyback style and she wrapped her legs around his waist to hold on.

"Are you serious?" she asked, nibbling his ear as he walked them into the bedroom.

"Casey, stay out there for a minute, will you?" he called. He dropped Georgia onto the bed and pulled a little black velvet box out of his nightstand.

Dropping onto one knee, he looked up at Georgia and opened the box. "Casey helped me pick it out. She said you loved the huge pink sapphire engagement ring Nicole Richie got, so I had one made just like it."

"Holy shit."

"Is that a yes?"

"Um…you haven't asked me anything."

Jonathan jumped on the bed and straddled her, still holding the ring in his hand. "Will you marry me?"

"Yup."

He kissed her hard, and suddenly his cock was between her thighs, ready to go.

"Wow," she said. "Marriage must really turn you on."

"You turn me on," he murmured, filling her with one stroke, raining kisses down on her face as she circled her hips madly to meet his thrusts. "I love you, Sweet Georgia."

"Good," she said. "Because I love you too."

The End

ABOUT
SHOSHANNA EVERS

Critically-acclaimed author Shoshanna Evers has written dozens of sexy stories including Amazon Erotica Bestsellers *Overheated*, and *Enslaved, Book 1 in the Enslaved Trilogy*, as well as the post-apocalyptic dystopian *Pulse Trilogy* from Simon & Schuster Pocket Star. Her work has been featured in *Best Bondage Erotica 2012* and *Best Bondage Erotica 2013*, the Penguin/Berkley Heat anthology *Agony/Ecstasy*, and numerous erotic BDSM novellas including *Chastity Belt* and *Punishing the Art Thief* from Ellora's Cave Publishing.

The non-fiction anthology Shoshanna Evers edited and contributed to, *How To Write Hot Sex: Tips from Multi-Published Erotic Romance Authors*, is a #1 Bestseller in the Authorship, Erotica Writing Reference, and Romance Writing categories on Amazon.

Reviewers have called Shoshanna's writing "fast paced, intense, and sexual…every naughty fantasy come to life for the reader" with stories where "the plot is fresh and the pacing excellent, the emotions…real and poignant."

Shoshanna used to work as a syndicated advice columnist and a registered nurse, but now she's a full-time smut writer and a home-schooling mom. She lives with her family and two big dogs in Northern Idaho.

Shoshanna Evers wants you to stay in touch!
Like erotic romance? Sign up for Shoshanna Evers's
mailing list to be notified when a new book releases—right
side of the page at ShoshannaEvers.com/blog

Visit **ShoshannaEvers.com**
for monthly giveaways and red-hot excerpts!

Let's be BFF's!
Twitter @ShoshannaEvers
Facebook/shoshanna.evers